Cheers, Vail

wo Sh   ")

Thank you to my edi   always
          g   struggle.

Here's mine
Enjoy,
Harrison
xox

One

I sat on the edge of his workshop cross-legged, thumbing through a ragged copy of Nation's Enhancements. The smoky burnt-solder air kept tugging at my focus until I finally gave up with the 'zine.

"This'll really work?" I said.

"Zach, my dear boy, absolutely, beyond a shadow of a doubt," he replied, as he twisted at a bolt lodged through the bridge of his nose. Each half a turn he'd suck in the air with a harsh sniff. I called him The Poet. I think on it now and it probably wasn't wise, but at the time it was justified. He began to gesticulate passionately as he wafted the air over a fresh rose.

"O lord of lords, of earthly woes and heavenly blessings! The olfactory of the gods is mine!" The smoke from his soldering iron had diffused and I could only just scent the rose. Nation's listed enhancements for olfactory at around £2,000 base price, which was ten years' salary at minimum wage. Those enhancements would allow your average creep – an unaltered human – to identify a molecule in part one of a million. The Poet's olfactory enhancement outperformed Nation's by five times and at half the cost. Why? He wasn't motivated by wealth or power. He wanted to expand, to encompass all and from that high mountaintop, describe what he saw.

"Listen," I said, twiddling my thumbs. "I've got to go. Great job on it – just remember to eat, yeah?"

He nodded with his eyes tightly shut. Trying to deduce every scent in the room. I donned my jacket and lit up a joint, then headed out into the rain.

I want to make it clear that it wasn't my choice to be a creep. There is this genetic abnormality, leaving a small subset of the populace who can't be 'wired up.' In most people the point in the brain that's jacked is coated in a mucus layer that insulates – it's a cell adhesive, the protein encoded by a gene called alphaflem. It stops leaky electrons from zapping your brain into a steamy puddle of pink and grey when loaded with enhancement gear. I, unfortunately, belong to the group who don't have the mucus. I don't have the gene. I'm the drudge that crawls behind the altereds. The creeps of Earth are doomed to be wiped from history.

I made the short walk from the workshop to my office building. The joint's ash flicked off in the wind and singed my hand. Our bodies wither and die with no stabilizing nano protoplasm to boost cellular growth and repair; everything hurts.

I looked up just as sunlight slipped through a crack in the clouds, and my eyes were scorched and stunned by the UV. Our eyes degrade over time without UV films and bio-lenses.

In frustration I kicked a flower from its stem, slipping on the wet ground and slamming onto the pavement. Our bones grow brittle, snap and crack without platinum-titanium nano coatings.

All this suffering I have to endure because of one shitty recessive gene. One shitty allele that my parents didn't fancy passing down. What's even worse is the cost-effective nature of the economy. If mankind put the resources into it, I'm sure we could have spliced the gene into the zygote. But point four per cent of nine billion just wasn't worth it. Wasn't a big enough pot.

I arrived at work with the roach of my joint gripped tight between my lips. I sucked out what was left and spat the thing to the ground.
"You're late," a voice called from the window above.
I looked up with a grimace and spotted my boss, Mr Matheson. Matheson was a creep like me. His wife had left him on the second night of their honeymoon. She'd run off with a Brazilian tongue dancer, who'd supposedly been in trials for porn star-quality penile enhancements. Nation's didn't list those, sadly. I walked up the circular staircase to my floor. Matheson was standing there lecturing some poor sod about holocopier protocol. I managed to slip by and headed for my desk.
There was very little work for creeps these days. Most creeps had IQs of
100. The average IQ of an altered was 160. If you were lucky you might find work in a creative industry: writer, artist, filmmaker etcetera. IQ didn't seem to have much effect on creativity, only its implementation. So they'd often team a creep who'd scored a high CQ with an altered who'd scored poorly. There were some wonderful works that came out of pairings like this, but it was rare.

A looming shadow darkened my desk. I swivelled my chair to face the source, lo! It was Matheson.

"Late again, Mr Blue."

I shrugged him a response and spoke as softly as I could. "I'm sorry, Harry. I was with my grandfather. He's … losing the battle." Matheson paused for a moment as if his creep mind needed time to process communication.

"I'm sorry to hear that. He's an eccentric, your grandfather, I hope one day to meet him."

I tried to swerve the chair back as nonchalantly as possible. Matheson grabbed the backrest and leant forward.

"The Bio Enhancement Board is on my case," he said in a hushed tone. "They want your report and they are getting impatient. Why are you still here? You should be at the testing facilities."

I worked for a small creep division, part of a government body that regulated bio enhancements: manufacture, trade, use, the list went on. If bio enhancements were involved, we'd be in the background.

"Mappo's put out another forty-five testing calls for pures. And what's worse, they want 700 pitifuls," Matheson said. "Mappo's claiming to have 'the cure'." He gestured air quotes.

Creeps are often used for testing. Pures are the real minority: a philosophical movement based around purity. A pure has made the choice to actively not upgrade him or herself, lots of willpower.

"They want pitifuls?" I said, rising from my chair.

"That's right, the board hasn't got a clue what's going on. You ask me, Zach, Mappo are power drunk. They've sat at the top for too long. The prime minster is apparently trying to push some new laws on corporate monopolies. Ever since Bio-Tee-Cee left the game…" Matheson shook his head. "Well you know how it is, every one's jacked with Mappo gear."

And then there's a pitiful creep like myself. Our genes are trash.

Pures are massively valuable to a bio enhancement manufacturer. They can test on the creep and have no worries about interference from other enhancements – a fresh canvas.

I gestured to the coffee machine. Matheson nodded and followed me over.

"I'm not there as I'm not done with my initial report. Mappo Corp isn't known for its catch-all safety procedures." I handed Matheson his coffee.

"Thanks," he said. "I still want you to pose as a pure. I think this pitiful testing call is a load of hot air. Mappo are flexing, maybe the new neural nets are coming out and they want some free advertisement. I dunno. Oh and since when did you care about your life?"

I sipped at my coffee; the hot mocha burnt my tongue. His dead eyes bored into mine.

"I'll leave tonight. Give me a little more time and the board will have their report."

Two

I headed east from the city centre. The train approached the platform silently, floating on a bed of air. I stepped in and took the closest seat I could, but as soon as I sat, I lunged forward and let out a yelp. I turned to see a metal tentacle with a fine needle point jabbing at the air with frantic desire.

"Sorry, sir, looks like you're in the wrong area," an attendant said.

I was motioned into the creeps-only passenger carriage and secured a seat next to a window, tentacle-free. Why would you want to plug in anyway? The view was half the point. But Then what did I know? I didn't have a clue what I was missing.

I took out my notepad and flicked through to my most recent jottings. This wasn't the first time I'd posed as a pure creep. I'd done it before back in '32 and then once again in '35. The only thing that had changed was the detection method for the mucus allele, alphaflem. In the past, testing was done with a full genome mapping and what's called a tester file. They'd take your blood and keep your genome on a big server. Say they never got round to testing on you or removed the gear from you, then your file got marked as pure. You could go test again. So I found a way to alter the file and mark it as pure, then sold my program to a few people, making a little on the side. This ended horribly when one guy ended up getting his brains zapped at Bio-Tee-Cee.

It was getting late and the rain continued to pour. A hazy fog started to roll in over the hills as the train track cut through. I was heading to New Peak District City: a bastion for green technology. An eco-friendly mixing pot where old age venture capitalists would go out hunting for green gold. The amount of innovation and improvement made since the wave of bio enhancements first broke was astounding. Earth and most notably England led this green stampede. Terraformed colonies too – Mars and her moons then Jupiter's moon, Europa – all followed this path of enlightenment. The enhancements allowed humans to think clearly for the first time in their existence. Building sustainable infrastructure: power, water, food and rare elements. It worked like the innards of an intricate mechanical clock, civilisation – what a thing. The only downside was the creeps. The creeps were the smudge on the canvas. One that was soon to be erased.

The train stopped at a station equidistant from London and New Peak District City. A slender woman boarded and sat opposite me. She had deep pools for eyes, green like opals that swirled if you stared for too long. I spoke laconically, like The Poet had taught me.

"Zach." I held out my hand. She looked me up and down, and then shook it firmly.

"Autumn." She spoke so softly, like a whisper. I wasn't sure how best to move forward, drowned in my thoughts of self-doubt.

"Where you headin'?" She had a strange accent – Australian or American.

"Docklands, NPD City." Laconic keys will unlock a woman's heart. I could hear The Poet's passionate idioms eddying in my mind. I dragged my hand over the map display – pinned up on the carriage wall beside me – across to Docklands station. "Yourself?"

"Docklands Station? Well, looks like you'll be stuck with me for a while."

She was definitely American.

"Work or play?" I said.

"Work – well, hopefully, I'm plannin' on bein' a tester for Mappo. They've got a manufacturin' plant not too far from the station. It's tough times for us creeps." She spoke with a melancholy undertone. If I had to guess, she was a purist. I don't think you could upgrade her. Flowing black hair, angular features and a pale, milky complexion. She was my ideal.

"And what are you doin' out at Docklands?" She seemed sincere in her questioning.

"Work also, in fact I'm going out to Mappo too."

In my line of work knowing who to trust was the key skill that sorted who remained employed and who didn't. If you got caught passing off as a purist it was prison. And if you didn't break from the testing soon enough, then your brain was zapped, like my power friend at Bio-Tee-Cee. That's why you needed an in-man who'd let you loose once you'd collected your data.

"Oh! Well let's hope they've got spots for the both of us."

I cracked a smile in response, wary of her motives.

Passing through the penultimate station, Autumn and I were midway through a game of holochess. She was crafty and agile. She thought with rash logic and still played dangerously. I had to succumb to her: in a valiant last attack on her queen my last rook was captured. Then, like slaughtering helpless chickens, my pieces were taken, and I was checkmated. I smiled and slouched back into my seat. Her IQ and CQ were most definitely higher than mine. At the time I thought it was a minor issue, a footnote for a much larger work. The power of hindsight.

"Docklands Station approaching. End of the line," the conductor bellowed through the speakers.

Three

"You headin' over to the plant then?" Autumn said, glancing up the road.

"They're taking testers all night," I said. "Food?"

The flicker of a neon sign in the puddle beneath my feet caught my attention as I failed to work my lighter. My hand felt number than usual trying to get the flint to spark. I rubbed an eye with my free hand and chalked the added numbness up to fatigue.

"Here let me." She plucked the lighter from my hand. "You've just gotta have that … magic touch." And with that, an incandescent flame of orange, yellow and blue birthed from the lighter. She held it under my cigarette as I drew a breath.

"You've got to be the last man on Earth who smokes these."

I nodded and exhaled smoke, trying hard to not blow any into her face. We walked towards the diner just as the clouds began to spit.

A burly, big-busted woman of about forty approached our booth and spoke with a raspy voice.

"What can I … uchummm … can I get the two of you?" Her beady eye darted between us in ever-increasing frequency. The other eye – a Mark IV Opi-Tech Iris – had a deep red glow with small half-inch metal discs that rotated as it focused. She was bubbling up with something. "You two getting married?"

"No ... er, no. Of course not," I said. Autumn winked at me and my face flushed a bright red.

"Lots of couples in town, wedding fair," the waitress said.

"I'll ... hemm ... I'll have a green tea and ... ah-hemm ... a full English." My throat was tight and dry. Like gargling with a mouthful of sand.

"Coffee and a pancake please," said Autumn.

The waitress ambled off with our order.

"Will this be your first time testing?" I said. Her eyes locked with mine and she stiffened, withheld breath then finally spoke.

"No, I ... I did once have somethin' you could call a career. But that fell apart when the spinal enhancements came out. Ever since then it's been testin'." She looked down at the table, her hands fiddling with a scrap of gunk left from the last diner's meal.

"What was your career?" I asked.

She smiled and brought her gaze upon me once more.

"I was a dancer, ballet," she said.

My fists balled under the table. My heart rate started to rise, knowing that the altereds had taken that from her. We were being scrubbed out systematically.

The food arrived promptly, the smell of Autumn's coffee and pancake winning me over. I looked down with reproach at my full English and began eating.

We'd finished the meal, paid and left in under an hour. I started to take comfort in Autumn's presence. She seemed a flicker of hope in an otherwise lost cause. We made our way to Mappo's facility under the moonlit sky. The dense rain clouds that loomed earlier had vanished, leaving behind a calm, starry night. I felt an urge to hold Autumn's hand as we walked side by side. She'd smile and laugh as I bathed in the radiant magnanimity I'd assigned her.

Mappo was located in the centre of town, about a mile from the diner and station. It took us two hours to walk there. The slow pace I attributed to deep and wondrous conversation.

Large guards with huge mechanical arms and legs hurried us in. Fixed to their wrists were concentric rings of barrels. Attached, ran belts of large bullets that fed from boxes fixed to the guards' backs. Their helmets covered the entirety of their heads, fronted by glass or Perspex visors, which – as far as I could tell – displayed neon green HUDs of information. They were more machine than human.

Troves of creeps had turned up for the testing and a restless crowd had formed. They looked like they'd been out of work for a while: ragged clothes, messy hair, malnourished physiques.

"Proceed down the road," one of the guards said in a monotone. He was gesturing to a tent. Autumn and I started to walk, when a large hand grabbed her by the shoulder.

"What are you doin'?" she screamed.

"Women are to be sent this way." She must have been ripped six feet from the ground. I stopped but was quickly pushed away by another guard. I caught a glimpse of her eyes, as wide as the moon.

We were marched down into the tent and stripped of our clothes. My thoughts clung to Autumn; I could feel my legs twitching, my heart rate rising. My body was burning with desire to run to her. But I needed this. If Mappo could do what they promised, I'd be a creep no more.

A cold, searing pain ripped through my body, as about fifty others and I were power washed. Small autonomous drones illuminated the tent. They would fly down, dock to a person's shoulder and take blood from the neck. Horrible things about a third of a foot in diameter, a full sphere of chrome and neon blue.

It was at this point I began to wonder what I'd got myself into. I was a pitiful creep. No matter what, I could never be upgraded. But Mappo had raised suspicions when they published papers on the SYX-Serum. It would alter a person at the most fundamental levels. Turning them into putty to be moulded, shaped and then cooked hard once more. It was normal for blood to be taken, but Mappo's sophistication was unmatched and I feared I would be snuffed out before I could verify their claims.

The drones zoomed out, whipping up the tent's flaps as they left. A short but well built man wearing a white suit and green shirt appeared, and gestured to the shivering bodies in front of him. As one we silenced and stared in awe.

"Thank you for being here." He spoke with a mollifying tone, neither too soft nor too harsh. "Without you, Mappo wouldn't be the company – nay! – the revolutionary it is today. You're the first of what I hope to be the last generation of creeps to ever walk this earth."

He must have been sixty, sixty-five. He leant on a walking stick as he took a step closer to us.

"I will eradicate this plague, one creep at a time. And we will be as one, finally united."

Moments after he left the tent, two mechanical guards came in and began chucking transparent bags of clothing at us.

"Change!"

Four

"Zach … Zach are you in there?" whispered a voice.

I pulled myself from the bed and peered through my haze at an imperfect seal in the door.

"Xavier?"

"Yeah, oh thank fuck I found you. We've got to go. Step back from the door."

I took a couple of shaky paces backwards. About to finish the third step when an intense blast threw me backwards. My feet shot out from under me and I landed on my bed, shielding my face from licks of flame and debris.

"What the fuck are you doing?" a voice that sounded like mine screamed, my ears ringing with ferocity.

"Let's go!" he shouted.

I'd been locked up in Mappo's facilities for thirty-four days. Heavily sedated, I was unaware of the time that slipped by. We snuck from Mappo's grasp and took solace in Xavier's home. He lived just on the outer ring of New Peak District City, burrowed deep in a snow-capped mountain. My palms sweaty and shaky I motioned to Xavier for a cigarette. He hunted around and found a crumpled pack amid a stack of journals.

"Here, sit," he said, lighting the thing for me. I took a pull from a glass of water then a drag from the cigarette. It went like that for a while.

"What the fuck is going on?"

"War," Xavier said.

"War?"

He handed me his tablet and pressed Play.

Mappo Corp's continual assault on Phobos Prime has caused global political tensions to rise … Phobos Prime is mainly populated by New Soviets … The United Anglo Nations have come under pressure with England's Prime Minister, Adam Forrest, calling for mass globalisation of UAN and the New Soviet armies.

'This is what happens when private companies form monopolies,' said the Prime Minister in an interview with BBC News. 'Our resources for monitoring and controlling them aren't sufficient. More should have been done and now lives have been lost,'

The UAN and the Martian council are meeting later today in London. More to follow.

"Holy shit."

"Why did you go to Mappo?" said Xavier. My lip quivered as the taste of smoky, fetid air overcame me.

"I … What?"

"They found markers for alphaflem in you. Not just any markers but fundamental understandings or whatever nonsense. Now Mappo have the power to render any human, or anything really, completely unenhanceable."

I stood, dizzily walked a few steps then leant my head against the wall. A ball of pressure formed and bubbled up in my stomach. Salt-saturated saliva pooled in my mouth. The thickest of knots grew tighter inside of me. Then I wretched and heaved about a litre of thick brown-green mush into the waste bin at my feet.

"Autumn," I said, wiping my face with my arm.

"What?"

"Autumn – where is she?"

"She? Look, Zach, you're a wanted man. It took me about two weeks to realise what was going down and then another two to work out how to get you out. I got to your grandfather before they could. He's safe."

"Autumn!" My thoughts were like a ship anchored to rocks in too shallow water. Nothing would move them.

"I can get the manifests but if she was anything like you, a pitiful, then it's likely she wasn't let go. You remember our deal, right? I want him to do it for nothing now. And I want him to do it to me too."

"Fine. Just save her and take me to The Poe … take me to my grandfather."

Xavier ran a rag across my face and pulled my arm over his shoulder. He left me to sleep on the sofa. I slept a cold, sweat-soaked sleep, drugs slowly seeping out of my body.

"Boy!"

My eyes squinted as the light broke through the poorly tinted windows. A silhouette formed a shape I knew. A face.

"Boy, wake up," said The Poet.

I swivelled up from the sofa and rested my head in my hands. Xavier walked in with his daughter Ellie holding his hand, a teddy clutched by the paw in the other. She must have been five years old or so. She'd learnt to call me uncle and The Poet great uncle.

"It's good to see you." My lips cracked as they arched into a smile.

Xavier sat down next to me and laid out his tablet. The Poet stood motionless, his frayed, stringy white hair in contrast with the flushed red face.

"Are you going to say anything?" I said.

"I must perform the operation on Ellie and Xavier now if we don –"

There was a thump at the door. Xavier thrust the tablet into my hands and motioned to the kitchen.

"Out, take Ellie," he said, eyes darting like a crazed killer. "You have the tablet – as long as you have that I can reach you. Please do as you prom –"

The thumps came to a stop.

"Go, hurry." His breath was shallow and faint.

Tear gas canisters rolled in at our feet. I dragged Ellie and The Poet into the kitchen. As I slung her over my shoulder, she locked tight around my neck.

"Open it." I pointed to the trapdoor at our feet.

There was a small burst of laser fire. Then a tracer round bounced down through the hall and popped out through the kitchen door. Tear gas poured out of the newly-formed hole. I heard Xavier's muffled cries.

"Go," I said, pointing south down the passageway.

Five

We broke free from the mountain passage, arriving at the coast.

"How could you throw us into this?" The Poet said.

"Us?" I said.

This wasn't the first time I'd used The Poet's skills and savvy for favours. Back in '33 I had The Poet install custom eye mods for a Bio-Tee-Cee employee on the condition she let me into a privately run landfill site. Bio-Tee-Cee were shortly shutdown. The Poet's passion and skills were why I still had work. Without him I'd be less than nothing.

"Yes, us. You, the girl and I. All in this together. Through no fault of mine." His tongue hissed. There was a beautiful juxtaposition: the sun kissed the still calm sea, which reflected and sparkled all around versus the rampage we'd just avoided. Xavier gave his life for me. I never did forget him.

"We need to get to my workshop. There I can perform Ellie's operation."

I nodded and grabbed Ellie's hand. I'd run out of friends. My heart pulled me in one direction and my honour bound me to another.

```
--- MEMORY_LEAK_0xCCFF66 ---
    --- TRANSLATOR V. 3.3.1 ---
       © MAPPO CORP - 2275.
```

The Dialogues I

'Utopia?' said The Poet.

'No sense in cradling a foolish spirit,' Koshi replied.

'But Master, I believe in this. It's attainable; it's in sight. The technology I'm building now will fundamentally change the human condition, it will rewrite our most basic evolutionary instincts.'

Koshi paused and drew a long breath, then, 'Let me tell you a story, hmm?'

The Poet nodded.

'In the height of the Samurai of ancient Japan, a warrior became a ronin when his master was struck down by a bolt of lightning. The 雷-sama, eh! This poor ronin made off with his master's armour and sword then set out for vengeance. He was determined to bring the kaminari-sama to justice. But how does one scorch what is already on fire? How can one slay a god?'

The Poet waited for answers, his serenity devoured by curiosity. 'How?'

'Ah! There is no god, see? How long have you held that knowledge? To you or I it is simple we can perceive the nonsense that the poor ronin could not. He swore to the skies and heavens he would have justice.'

'My idea of utopia is like a ronin fighting a thundercloud?'

'Not only are clouds elusive, they have the tendency to take myriad shapes. Forming what the observer wants to see, not which is really there.' Koshi paused and poured sweet tea into their mugs. 'This ronin climbed the highest trees, scaled the tallest peaks. He waved his master's sword about, fighting fog. But the thunder still came. It roared with passion as Raijin, or 雷様 as the ronin would have screamed, banged his drums. He didn't give up. He built a new type of 弓, a yumi that required the archer to cut off his draw finger.'

'Cut it off? Am I to sacrifice myself to obtain utopia?' said The Poet.

'But the added range of the bow only flung the arrow deeper into the cloud. It neither stopped nor affected it in any great way.' Koshi sipped at his tea. 'The poor ronin was old now, father to a useless son, husband to a sick wife. He disfigured his son by removing his draw finger. More archers meant a greater chance of stopping Raijin. Not much later did he have the whole of his village shooting arrows into the skies, to strike down Raijin and bring justice. Ha! Do you see now? No? The samurai of the local area called the people of that village "愚霊". The apex of this is simple. Without true knowledge of what you are trying to create, you will never succeed. My question for you: what is your utopia?'

Six

Ellie is dead. The Poet couldn't save her. Xavier was a fool; he'd taken Ellie to a modder, someone much like The Poet, only far less skilful. He'd had the modder install a CQ unit. In both of them. As with most backend moddings it went horribly wrong. It decayed, leaked and then slowly poisoned her.

Ash flickered off into the wind. The tendrils of smoke from her burning corpse spiralled up like a stairwell to the heavens. Only she wasn't in heaven. She wasn't anywhere. Didn't exist. The Poet perched himself on the window's ledge facing the flames, the glow and reflection in his eyes iterating over some distant memory. Some long-lost wishful thinking. Vile thinking that landed us in this world.

"What now?" he said to me.

"We go find Autumn."

The Poet's face screwed up, his cheeks turning red.

"Not a moment to mourn? I raised you better than this!" His words were like acid to my face. But I swallowed it down. That sickening feeling you get when you know you're a contradictory piece of shit who probably got more than he deserved.

"I didn't know the girl!" I plucked a cigarette from my jacket's inner pocket. "You're the one who couldn't save her."

"I ... Boy, please, don't."

"Or what? What could you possible do to me that you've not already done?" And like that I was thrust into the window. Glass cracked and shattered, and the sharp scent of blood plumed into the air. I'd forgotten old Darwin's book had been rewritten. His vice-like grip closed on my throat. Words only just escaping the soon to be sealed.

"Grand ... dad ... please..." Tighter and tighter and tighter. "I..."

"How dare you test me?"

The bully you once knew was only human. Only so strong. Only capable of such feats. But now that bully has synthetic tendons and sinews. His bone is harder, denser. His reflexes faster. Outwitted, outgunned and outmatched.

The Poet let me loose. I coughed and croaked and lit the cigarette that was long overdue. I walked into the house and headed for the sofa but before I could reach it, a noise startled me. The vibration came from my satchel. Xavier's tablet. A private contact. I answered and the video instantly became live. The ghostly whitewash of the screen that was too intense at first slowly dimmed. And there she was. Gagged and bound. My stomach knotted, as if pulled tight by giants.

"Mr Zachary Blue?" the tablet squawked.

"Autumn!"

"If you want to see her alive again, bring me Doctor Nicholas Blue. Bring him to the London Space Elevator Station. Tomorrow, 10.00pm."

It shut off.

"Mappo. Aged, but it's him," said The Poet, sneaking up from behind.

"Why does he want you?"

He gestured for me to sit. "I've not been honest with you. Not completely. You know me as an inventor, yes? As a radical? Before you were born, Elijah and I … we shared a vision. We knew we could build this world. We knew we could turn it into what it is now. We founded Mappo Corp. And we slaved away at it. Built the artificial neural nets first. Freed our thinking. But, Elijah, he had what burdens you. Alphaflem. No matter what methodology we adopted, we couldn't upgrade him. And over time he grew bitter. I became ill and we went our separate ways. Whatever he is up to now I do not know. Why he wants me I do not know."

I sank deeper into my chair. This pioneer was like me. Mappo was a pitiful-creep. A world-leading pitiful-creep. And if he could be part of the creation of this world, I could surely be part of its demise.

"I assume he's finally found a way around the alphaflem problem and needs me to help implement it. But while he's waging this war he knows I would never help him willingly."

"I must take you to him," I said. "Autumn means a lot to me."

He met my gaze; I stood my ground and bored into his eyes. This wild sense of belonging, a raw passion I'd never had the pleasure of experiencing. Finally understanding the motives behind the crimes of passion, the insane acts of love. To march and to go to war, for love, for her.

"We get in, get her and we get out. I won't be a piece in this campaign of madness Elijah wants to play," he said. 'Campaign of madness' was an astute assessment. My hand extended out, palms sweaty with fear. We shook hands; I dozed what was left of the night.

Laid out on the sofa from the corner of my eye I could see him. Sitting, meditating. The Poet didn't sleep, drank about an eighth of what I needed, and ate even less. His body and mind didn't need resources like mine. He was an altered. Didn't know true hunger or the crazed tortured thoughts of a sleep-deprived soul. It was this harsh edge, such a distinct split in a race of beings, which elicited my hatred. He was post-human, evolved beyond mere flesh and bone.

My mind wandered to Autumn, her soft rose cheeks. Those eyes of forest green. And she wasn't like The Poet. She was a creep. She was like me.

Morning came swiftly, sunlight breaking through in scattered hues. The numbing of my hand had worsened; I could barely feel the ridges in my lighter's spin-wheel. From my satchel I pulled a thin mechanical cylinder, about the size of those archaic pens from once upon a time. The shooter was designed to fire tiny synthetic cells into my bloodstream. From there the cells gather up glucose and swell in size, converting the chemical energies into mass and tissues used to repair the sheath that insulates my nerve cells. You see, if I could be altered I could simply have the endoneurium and perineurium sheaths replaced totally with a nanofibre weave. Instead I have to scrape what I can together to afford a small dosage of the blasted stuff that's coursing around me now.

The Poet walked in, nodding towards the door.

"Let's make this quick," he said sharply. No sense of empathy or compassion. "I want to elucidate, this is the last time I help you, Zach. Take the benefits from the state. Marry this girl and live a good life. What do you have, seventy years? You don't know, maybe Mappo's tech can be salvaged once the UAN are done with them. Maybe we can finally rid the world of the creep – sorry, unaltereds."

"I don't need hand outs. I'll survive off the burn from my own back."

"Stubborn, like your father."

I made the habit of tuning The Poet out.

At the front of the house we waited. A small device on The Poet's wrist, I think they're called synaptic-taps, flashed red neon, then yellow, then green. A hole, about the diameter of a manhole cover, opened up on the ground. Slowly a platform rose, on it a black monolith. About as tall as The Poet, as thick as my wrist. It stood, waiting. The Poet tapped twice on the synaptic-tap. The monolith dissolved into a cloud of darkness. Shifting and changing, no sound. After about five seconds a bike stood before my eyes. A motorcycle, with huge white-rimmed wheels. Muted chrome metal and the words, 'utopia atque libertatem' engraved into the side. He jumped on. The engine, like the sound of compressed air being forced through an intricate web of pipework, howled and rattled. My body shook from the depths of the unknown. The Poet wasn't just a creator of society: he was a god.

He pulled out a band and wrapped it around his temples. From there the band protruded and encompassed his head. A visor covered his eyes and lit up, informing him of speed and directions.

"When did you build this?" I asked, incredulous.

"I've been working on it a while, my boy. She's a true machine. Can take on any form, you see? I will meet you at the station. I have errands to run. If Elijah wants me, and is willing to go to war for me … I fear he's lost his mind. I will help you find her, Zach, don't worry."

I nodded as he jetted off. The thin trail of vapour from his bike diffused into the air.

I needed to ensure I still had my job once all this hell was over. I needed to speak with Matheson.

Seven

"Zach!" the big-breasted buffoon of a man exclaimed as I walked in. "Good to see you. We were getting worried, there's lots of work to be done." His face was full and alive – flustered but alive.

"What work would that be? Mappo's declared war on all off-Earth colonies. Surely the board doesn't need the report?"

He sat me down, resting a daring hand on my knee.

"Military contracts, not just any old regular stuff, they're pushing us harder than before. Because of this mess with Mappo Corp, the UAN wants us to front a new organisation, preventing misuse and monopolies, only this time – with force. We've been given access to exosuits too; combat training. The whole deal."

He was shaking; smiling like he'd just found out he wasn't a creep. You could see the glimmer of hope in his eyes. It wasn't going to bring back his wife, or any kind of peace. Many people forced themselves into waging a wayward pursuit after being so fundamentally hurt. Signing off on a rushed-through military gig was about as wayward as you could get. But, having access to an exosuit – about the only thing creeps had in the battle against the altereds – well, that was a nice surprise.

"The suits? Are they here?" I said.

"Arrived the other week, why?"

"Where?"

There was something about fine engineering, the way everything came together. This harmony of interwoven complexities, birthed from the fundamental laws of nature. Spliced with quality to provide a solution for a problem. It was the ultimate endeavour. To chip away at the unknown and solve something.

The suits stood at eight foot tall, yellow like the sun with patches of black. At the joints there was a twist of fibres, like looking at raw muscle.

"System, Zero-Zero-One, activate." The thing lit up. "System, new combatant." It cracked open and lowered itself. I stepped in, feeding my arms and legs into the holes inside. The immense power – oh, to be an altered.

"What are you doing?" cried Matheson.

"Just borrowing it," the suit growled in a robotic, omnipotent tone, "you'll get it back."

```
--- MEMORY_LEAK_0x66CDFF ---
--- TRANSLATOR V. 3.3.1 ---
     © MAPPO CORP - 2275.
```

The Dialogues II

Can an observer ever see objectively?
A question that had puzzled The Poet for a long time. He pushed and prodded from a variety of angles, disciplines and philosophies. He concluded that the subjective wrap — you or I would call a 'self' a 'you' or an 'I' — are in fact, senseless. Senseless is an interesting word to land on — notice the figurative speech? Land on, ha! The Poet understood that senseless words and sentences such as, 'you' or 'am I real?' do exist, and while our language and grammar allow for such an expression to be interpreted and superficially understood, it doesn't stop to verify the grandiose claim of its validity.

    The problem he was trying to solve was outlined in his paper, The Methods of Replication of Consciousness. It was in this paper he demonstrated the issue with what's known as 'the hard problem of consciousness'. He snubbed it up to a language issue: 'In such senseless endeavours of philosophers and neuroscientists, one must step back and recognise our introduction of senselessness, our qualia.' He did away with the issue by simply saying it was senseless. But not only was his language astute, he showed the nature of panpsychism.

It was a new phase for the word. He showed that any complex system, be it a wet mass of neurons or silicon or carbon, could be 'encoded' with a state called 'conscious-ready', then the process of panpsychism would occur. It was believed for a long time that when you 'uploaded' or 'copied' a mind to a computer system, you would have a split in continuity. The computer program would see its body and think, 'Hey, that's me!' And the mind in the body would think, 'Hey, that program thinks like me!' But an astounding process happens. Their 'consciousnesses' 'fuse' into a single mind or soul or self or you or I. The program senses what the body touches or tastes or smells, as does the mind in the body. The mind in the body also senses what the program feels or computes or sees.

They are as one.

Eight

The sun was sinking over the London Space Elevator Station. The carbon scrubbers took to the twilight like crazed fireflies. These blimps of the night cleared out the carnage left behind by dogmatic minds. Pre-altered minds.

Crouched with the suit's mask flipped open, my breath turned paper-white. The sting of cold air dulled in the adrenaline-infused moment. We were waiting for Mappo to arrive.

The monumental structure of interwoven cables of nanofibres that spanned to the upper reaches of space stood in front of us, looming, towering. A small cabin, buckled tight to the cables, descended. The silhouettes of exosoldiers merged into a messy black mass of machine and man as the cabin came closer. Slowly an outline of five made itself known. With a hiss the cabin landed.

"Stay hidden, boy," said The Poet. Pensive and tense, his tight, unmoved focus forced itself to bear deeper into uncertainty.

A pear-shaped man, cane in one hand, limped from the cabin. Shadowed by his exosoldiers, he raised a balled hand.

"Find them," he said.

An exosoldier, eight foot tall and covered in oily black metal lined with green neon, sank to his knees. From this stance an array of tiny floating spheres the size of golf balls bobbled and bloomed from his back. From each of them a wild laser show pierced the twilight.

"Seekers," said The Poet, with a hushed tone. "Power that suit down. I'll go and see what this fuss is about before –"

"Look!" I said.

She stepped from the cabin, an enigmatic expression on her face. She was as beautiful as the day I met her.

An internal whirling boomed. The lasers from the seekers all oriented to a single point. A pinprick on my forehead. The whirling grew to its crescendo; the armour suits lighting up in a crimson spectacle. The mask flipped down to cover my face, a ball of twisted fibre formed at my palm materialising into a curved, two-sided blade of black metal and white hot light – the tip of the metal bitten as if by a shark, leaving a serrated edge. My grip tightened, my heart raced, beads of sweat rolled from my brow. With unrelenting haste I attacked wildly. Seekers swooped and fired volleys of laser. Each strike a shooter-stab.

But there she was, standing, radiant.

"Boy!" cried The Poet.

I hacked and rampaged until I reached her, the seekers futile. Then exosoldiers descended upon me. Laser cannons for some, others solid matter rounds. They came thundering down, shot after shot. Like being strapped to the end of a fishing rod. Shaken. Rattled. Her image faded and slowly the signal in the visor lost its power. Then blackness.

Footsteps. Thud, thud, thud.

The hissing and crackling of broken electronics, the squalid smell of burnt nanofibre. My mask was pulled from me. A set of red robotic eyes peered into mine.

"Where is Nicholas Blue?" the exosoldier boomed.

"I … I … Who?" I whimpered, blood dripping from the corner of my mouth. It grabbed me by my throat, its cold hard fingers like clamps.

"Dr Nicholas Blue," it roared.

The others were closing in around me. Mechanical noises whined as the monsters moved in, the unsettled nature known all too well to me. I couldn't do anything to stop them. That limp will.

"He's here … Please … Bring Autumn."

The machine signalled to her. From behind Mappo she glided. Her essence a cushion of joy for my worn self to rest upon. My eyes began to turn turgid. She smiled a wry smile.

"Where is Dr Blue, Zach? Tell us," she said.

Us?

Stems of lightning rained down on the exosoldiers. Their lifeless bodies fell to the ground as if their souls ascended to the heavens.

"Mappo! What do you want?" called The Poet from behind me. His hands gripped around a fallen seeker.

"Ah! Nicholas," Mappo said, hobbling forward. "It's been so long." His gait an uneasy pedal, a self-imposed eminence of the highest honour.

"Boy, stay down," said The Poet. Autumn just stood there, like a machine, motionless, thoughtless.

"What do you want with me?" The Poet demanded as he marched towards Mappo.

"What I've always wanted from you Nicholas: cooperation." Mappo held out his hand. "You look tatty with that bolt in your face – never did have a firm sense of fashion." The Poet shrugged it off as Mappo continued, "That was a nice trick you played with the seekers. Come back to the firm."

The Poet swung with fervour, smashing Mappo's head with the seeker. Mappo yelped and slammed into the ground.

"Let's go. Autumn, I presume?" said The Poet.

Nine

It wasn't lust or loneliness. It wasn't any of those things. She was everything I could have dreamed of. But this person. This thing lying in front of me right now, this wasn't her. This wasn't the girl I fell in love with.

She was back with me, together forever.

"Are you just going to stare at her?" said The Poet.

Autumn was sprawled out on the sofa. Sound asleep. He gestured to the wall with one hand and held an index finger over his mouth with the other. A muted video feed came live. A ticker ran along the bottom overlaid on combat footage of Phobos Prime:

BREAKING NEWS: PM Forrest and the Martian council have declared war on Phobos. All civilians to evacuate to city safe zones.

"Are you reading this?" I said, turning my head and looking back. He took a moment to recognise my stare.

"I don't understand it. I –" He was cut short, a thump at the door.

"Mappo's exos?" I said.

"The alarms would have gone off." He paused. "Well go, open it."

"UANF. We are looking for Doctor Nicholas Blue," said a stocky woman with peroxide blonde hair and sea-coloured eyes.

"Can I see some IDs?"

The man behind her clicked at his wrist and a hologram popped up. UAN Forces ID and badge. Blondie did the same.

"Once you're in you can relay the information back to us," said Detective Mary King.

"We wouldn't have asked you to do this if you didn't have a military background. But – "

The Poet cut Detective Randall Jenkins off. "That was a long time ago. I've a family now." A quick glance over to me and he bored back into Jenkins' eyes. "I'd like to keep it that way."

The Poet had taken the olfactory bolt out of his nose. You could see from the incessant kneading of his thigh it was troubling him. I heard a creak from behind me and there she stood. Blondie and Jenkins' voices faded out as Autumn let out a yawn. Small pearls for teeth, soft thin red lips. Slight curves at the waist.

"Sleep well?"

"Zach?" Cluelessness fell upon her. "Zach? Is it really you?"

I smiled and nodded, stood and embraced her. She tiptoed to plant a kiss on my cheek. The Poet and the detectives were speechless, silent in awe of her beauty.

"Zach," said The Poet, "you two have some talking to do. Go. Out back."

The Poet's garden was filled with root vegetables and rare flowers. In the back was a bench swing that faced a pond. Shaped like the interior of an infinity sign, it housed freshwater fish. A small spider drone about the size of a tennis ball stood patiently waiting on the edge of the pond. Its gangly wire legs twitched whenever they felt a vibration. A dark cat with white speckles like flecks of paint crept up to the pond. The drone leapt at the cat, chasing it over to Autumn and me on the swing bench.

"Here kitty," Autumn said, grabbing the cat. "It's okay, the nasty bot won't get you now."

"Do you remember anything?" I said. The cat purred, contented and paid no attention to the spider drone waving its legs at our feet.

"No, not really. Flashes, my head hurts, a throb – strange dreams."

"I'm sure it'll get better," I said. "I think I love you," Fracture number one.

"Zach! What on Earth? It's nice to have a friend. But … You don't even know my last name, or where I'm from!" The cat leapt at the spider drone, letting out a gurgled screech. They tumbled into the pond – more screeches and cries.

"Then let me find out. We can settle down, we can go anywhere."

"I want normality, whatever that is. I came to England to start again, with worn-out sinew," she said.

I went to hold her hand, she shuffled away sitting on the corner of the bench. Those green eyes like Medusa's, they'd turn any man to stone. Frozen solid with fear that they might not get the chance to see her again.

"There it is, the wry smile. What is that?" I said. She stopped dead, only the noise of the spider drone being torn apart by its feline nemesis, its little legs going like pistons. Her breathing became calmer than ever. Like someone had just smashed her reset button.

"Autumn?"

"Zach, just leave me alone for a moment, would you please?" she said with that fucking wry smile. The poor little drone had its legs torn off. Sparks flew as I left her on that swing bench. That person I loved.

Blondie, Jenkins and The Poet were still sitting around the dining room table. The wall screen had a live satellite feed of Phobos Prime – the city was in ruins.

"The mag-film is leaking atmosphere and about forty per cent of the city's safe zones can't sustain their own," Jenkins said, pointing to the large complex. "This, here, is where we think Phobos's administration are. Adam Forrest's daughter is believed to be with them." The satellite image bloomed a bright white as a hot speck crashed to the ground. "We think Mappo are after Phobos's spaceport," Jenkins continued, as he scrolled the satellite images to a hollow cavern. "They made a rather large bid three years ago for it, which was rejected by the Martian council. What they wanted? Hell if I know."

The Poet looked vapid, eyes still and watery.

"What do you want with us?" I said.

"You? Nothing. We only need your grandfather. Ah yes, and the stolen and – I presume – broken exosuit. You'll be fined and fired. If your grandfather agrees to help us, we've negotiated a deal to have prison time reduced. You're reckless, Mr Blue, utterly reckless," said Jenkins.

"Prison?" I said.

"Part of the reason we came here, Mr Blue," said Blondie. "You're under arrest." Jenkins rose. The Poet's vapidity evaporated. My legs wobbled.

"Pri-son?" I said, my voice breaking.

"I'm sorry, Zach, it's all I could get for you. Once this ordeal is over, things will be right," The Poet muttered.

Suddenly everyone was standing, breathing deep heavy breaths. I could feel my blood flowing in and around me. The arteries on my neck swelling and ebbing. Beads of sweat forming at my shirt's collar.

"Whatever you're thinking, Mr Blue, we heavily advise you come with us willingly and don't protest," said Blondie.

That's the thing, there's only one creep prison in all of England. That's all they need. Low security by the sea. I couldn't have resisted even if I wanted to. Blondie could have ripped me apart without a moment's hesitation. Autumn coasted into the room, her mouth agape as if to speak, only to be stunned mute by the situation.

"Ah, Autumn. Zachary, Detectives Jenkins and King were just leaving," The Poet said, motioning to each of us with a swoop of his arm.

"After you, Mr Blue, transport's waiting outside," said Jenkins. The fucking smug cunt.

I turned to Autumn. She was cradling something in her arms. The Poet walked over and rested a hand on my shoulder.

"We'll get through," he said. "We'll get through." He stepped back as Autumn came forward. She laid the spider drone on the table and flung her arms around me. She'd deduced what was going on in a moment's notice. The Poet plucked the drone from the table.

"I've never seen this guy in better shape. Meaning to get to it. Fine work even for those with the gen elevens. When did you have your neural net installed, Autumn?"

Fracture number two.

Ten

I was taken from The Poet's home in London to the creep haven in Brighton. An old pavilion palace, retrofitted to be a prison. It housed 148 creeps. All dumb enough to break laws in a world where they were nothing but roaches. We were lucky in some ways … lucky not to have been squashed.

The cells were more like playrooms – we had access to wall screens and the excanet. Live streams from the outside. None of us could interface with it so they ended up giving us physical input devices – keyboards, mice etcetera. My cellmate, Snappy he went by, sat on the corner of his bed. The cell door in front of him had a narrow slit of Perspex.

"What are you doing?" I said.

"Tr … tryin … trying … to see the sea," he blurted out, fighting to keep the ticks at bay.

The first day I arrived I was moved into Snappy's cell. He'd been victim to a modder. That was a week ago now.

"You hear that, Snap? Door's unlocking, let's get some air."

Our cell door buzzed with a flash of green, swinging open. We walked down the steel gangway. The prison had huge windows for the ceiling, sea views for those on our level. Our boots clunked as we descended the spiral staircase. A prigd – what we called the prison guard drones – nodded at us as we headed outside. The prigd was big like Mappo's exos. Only these things were autonomous AI. Not human at all.

Snappy and I sat on a bench as close to the sea as we could get. The day was calm and the air sapid with salt. We listened to the sounds of waves crashing, gulls squawking. There was a strange beauty about prison. If you kept your nose clean, and paid attention to who to avoid, suddenly life became easy. Three meals a day, a bed, forced friends. It was kind of nice. The survival aspect was taken out of life.

"I don't know why I don't take the B I, Snappy."

"Buh ... B I?"

"Yeah, basic income, y'know, the state handouts. We get twice what the altereds get. We creeps."

"I'M NO CREEP!" he cried.

"Sorry, Snaps, I forgot. They just did such a seamless job on you it's hard to tell." You could see his face scrunch up. He wrapped his arms around his shoulders and let out a long breath.

A crunching sound grew louder, footsteps on gravel, I turned to see a recognisable pear-shaped figure. It was Mappo.

"Mr Blue," he said. "So good to have found you."

This, I think, is fracture number three. I debate it now, but as I write this I think this was the turning of my tide. My decisions from here weren't really my own, guided by lust and love, by insecurity.

"Mappo?"

"That's right, Mr Blue, after your grandfather left me for dead I was shortly incarcerated. Brought here, while my war wages on Phobos." He indicated for Snappy and me to make space. We complied and he sat, wheezing as his arse touched the bench. He stank of acrid cologne and cigar smoke. The prison jumpsuit was slightly too small for him and clung to his overweight physique like cling film around lard.

"What did you do to Autumn?" I said.

"Ah, yes, all in good time, Mr Blue. We are the same, no? You and I - we are like kin. Born into a world that isn't fit for us. Mice among men." I nodded and he continued, "Yet, we are unfortunate enough to burn with desire to reach something greater. Naïve, one might say - reminds me of a fable from long ago, about an archer. More to the point, Mr Blue, we have the power to take humanity back. You and I can achieve things, together, as one. Starting with fixing your dear Autumn."

"So she's changed? She's an altered?" I said.

Mappo spoke with a softness I'd not heard before. "She's changed. She was a pure creep. Now a neural net is slowing growing inside of her - why, I can't imagine. Swapping out the wretched neurons for synthetics. Generation Elevens." With his index fingers he traced a cross then left a single finger extended.

"Yes, yes, I've seen the adverts."

"What you've not seen, I can assure you, is that these nets are the first to have a grace period. If you change your mind, in a dualistic sense, you can have the net undo all it's done."

I shuffled my weight as my leg went to sleep. "How long do we have?"

"We've got about ten days before the net hits the point of no return." My head fell into my hands. As I sat slouched, Snappy put an arm around me, tightly gripping my shoulder. A tear rolled down my cheek and splashed into the ground, sucking up all the dirt and grit as it dried.

"My dear Mr Blue, your melancholy is misplaced. We've two nights left in this hive." I shot upright, ears sharp to the sound of his voice. The sound of hope. I looked at him quizzically, my brow tense and uneasy. "Phobos is a mere spectacle, something to keep the UANF off me. Off the real prize."

"And that is?"

"In good time, Mr Blue, in good time. Two days, 3.00am, make sure you're up. And your cellmate over here," he turned his gaze to Snappy, "You're very lucky to have Mr Blue as a friend. Now, gentlemen, I bid you good day."

Mappo hoisted himself up, putting all his weight into his knees and then plodded off. "Two days, Snap, two days."

Eleven

Alarms screamed as prigds fought in a haze of dust and smoke. Laser fire bounced around in the darkness. Snappy and I stood above the night's fiasco, leaning over the gangway railing. On my right about five prigds marched forward in the shape of an arrow. To the left, at the base of the stairwell, a jumble of exos and seekers – Mappo's private army. Waves of light swelled and ebbed as laser fire flew through the haze. A burst of green neon slammed into the leading prigd, a smouldering explosion of blue ink pouring from it as it collapsed to the floor. The fluid smelt like motor fuel, only more poignant – quicker to the senses.

Seekers whizzed around, sounds of mechanical purring filling the building. A seeker floated in front me, its lens about four inches from my nose. A spray of laser, slightly longer than a flash, emanated from the seeker's shell. It beeped and flew off, firing a burst into the haze. Glass fell from above, then a mechanical tendril dropped down, then another, and another. One wrapped itself around me, one around Snappy. The other still searching. A flurry of laser fire ripped Snappy's tendril; he fell, his face washed with fear and confusion. The haze swallowed him whole. I kept ascending.

Finally I reached a tricopter. Under each set of blades rested a housing for the autonomous tendrils. Mappo rose from the prison, gripped tight by the lifeless leviathan appendage. His eyes gleamed under the starlit sky, raw with audacity. The warmth of the rampage below had me sweating, leaking. Scared shitless.

Mappo's face cracked a wide ear-to-ear smile. The fiend I knew vanished before my eyes: he was now my saviour.

The tricopter landed us on the southern outskirts of London. It had flown over the rolling hills of the South Downs and kept a tight flight path, ensuring we were never detected. I vaguely recalled Mappo Corp owning an industrial unit out here. A manufacturing plant for exo gear. The tricopter's chassis popped open with a hiss of hydraulic fluid. It was about 4.00am, the coolness of the morning comforting after being locked up. A sense of freedom, of hunger for power surged from within. Elicited from Mappo's cavalier attitude; his willingness to ignore the fact he was outmatched.

"Quickly, Mr Blue, follow me," he said. I shouldered him to a gravel road. We made our way through what I assumed was a portion of Richmond Park. An exo rode up, inky black metal from head to toe. The crunching of gravel, the quiet hum of the engine – a buggy-type off-roader. All dark metal with neon lines at the folds of the panels, roofless apart from roll bars.

"Dr Elijah Mappo, 76OXYK-24," Mappo said. The exo looked him up and down, fired a spray of laser over him.

"Confirmed."

Mappo looked at me as he stepped into the buggy. "I'm sorry about this, Mr Blue."

Thud.

☐

```
--- MEMORY_LEAK_0x01FFEE ---
   --- TRANSLATOR V. 3.3.1 ---
      © MAPPO CORP - 2275.
```

The Dialogues III

You spend all your life trying to define who you are. What you stand for. When the reality is quite simple, you are nothing. Born from the dirt, back to the dirt you go. Life is the ultimate debt.

You borrow everything and give everything back. Koshi understood this, a teacher and a pupil of Qen. Koshi had learnt to let go of modern wants and cultural desires. Then there was 悟り. <TRANSLATION ERROR: CHARACTER NOT FOUND EXCEPTION!> A level of Qen fiercely sought after, many monks and holy people had spent lifetimes trying to attain it. Among the handful of Qen masters who had reached it was Koshi.

'Master, what is Qen?' said The Poet.
        'It is our connection, our objectification and subjectification of elsewhere. It isn't religion, nor is it science. It is everywhere; it is throughout. When you create something, when you stretch. This is Qen. It's the harmony of quality, the balance of action and inaction,' replied Koshi.

The Poet sank into a slouch, his brow constricted, watching as Koshi sat quiet and content knowing something he did not.

'How am I to understand if you do not teach?' he asked.

Koshi was seated slightly higher than The Poet. He was a short man, with tanned skin and a mouth full of small yellow teeth. He smelt like pine trees and had a bite to his voice. He would dig into syllables as if to play with the words, not for meaning's sake but for form. Random intonation and strange enunciation. Understanding what Koshi said was like being a master cipher cracker, trying fervidly to decrypt the gurgled mess. The temptation to give in was grand, to run off and do his own thing.

Ultimately The Poet was unsure. Was Koshi's view on Qen real? Did Qen really exist? Was this mindless rhetoric an indulgence of Koshi's? A babel straight from Koshi's ego. An ego that had twisted and devoured him long ago, leaving a hollow man who cared not for the truth, only for the affirmation of his Qen. Persistence was what it would take. With grand desires of creating a new world, a utopia, The Poet had to reach this level of universal understanding. A harmony just, in which The Poet's choices for mankind would lead down the road of enlightenment and not of darkness.

'I do teach; you do not listen. Quiet the storm, quiet the sceptical mind, quiet the curiosity. They are the Ox, no? They are the penultimate barriers. They are the anchors which keep you in aukkha.' Koshi smiled.

'How do I know what you say is real?'

'Real, synthetic, fake. Follow the path. Your path. If it isn't real, it won't matter. You will still be here, still be talking, accountable for actions, accountable for thoughtlessness. Walk the path and find out. I know you as someone who would not want to waste taken steps.'

The Poet nodded and swung down from his crossed-legged pose. He left.

Twelve

The salty taste of sweat, putrid breath and a dull aching head. My vision blurred, darkened by a patchwork of fabric, trace amounts of light scattered in. I couldn't feel my body, couldn't move my hands or feet. Breath was forced into me at a jarring rate, slightly too slow. Tricked into a false sense of asphyxiation. I heard the sounds of shuffling, of seeker drones buzzing, their mechanical whine reverberating all around me.

A rumbling sound followed by a whiteness, blooming intensity beyond my eyes' capabilities. A wall screen materialised in front of me. A voice first then an image. It was The Poet. My lips quivered. Unable to move my head, I could only just utter the word, "Grandfather."

A distinct hoarse voice boomed in from above me. It was Mappo.

"Nicholas, do what I say and he'll be fine. Returned to you in one piece. Don't do as I say and he'll stay like this." The horror I couldn't feel. I could only witness my predicament through the eyes of The Poet. That brief glimpse of sheer abhorrence. Raw eyes welling with tears for me and my situation. The wall screen cleared and Mappo stepped out, shouldered by an exo and a thin man with glasses, wearing a long white lab coat. The thin man bent down and looked into my eyes. I fought to keep them open. He rose and spoke.

"He's conscious, sir. I'm sorry, I thought he was out."

"Well knock him out then, he can't remember any of this!"

My drowsiness grew stronger, then nothing.

I woke in a hospital bed. The feeling of my extremities returned as I balled my fist and flexed my right arm. Hunger hugged my stomach. I turned in search of something to eat, and then I saw it. I stopped dead.

Through the window I could see Mars in all her beauty, turning effortlessly. She was a silent giant adrift in space. The left side of the planet was shrouded in darkness and from the darkness lights emitted, a city's worth. Concentric rings with darkness in between – the artificial canals of Tharsis. I swung my legs over the bedrail and walked up to the window. Resting my forehead on it, with each breath it grew translucent then a condensed white. I traced the lights of Tharsis in the window mist, wondering how all this happened. How I let things get so twisted and fucked. How once I found someone worth surviving for, worth enduring for, this world snatched her. Ripped her from me and mutilated her, turned her into a monster…

I heard a clunk. The door behind me bifurcated, each side sliding into its respective wall. A person stepped in, a heavyset person. Shifting all my weight onto my legs I spoke.

"Why?"

"I'm sorry about that, Mr Blue, we had to make it look real," said Mappo.

"That look in his eyes. You tortured him, tormented him. And for what?"

"Mr Blue, Nicholas has landed. He arrived at the Phobos Prime hangar four hours ago. What we did to you on Earth wasn't all for show – you are an essential piece in this game. Your body contains the alphaflem gene. But it also contains something else, something far greater. Something I've been looking for all my life. Your plasma cells manufacture an antibody, which attacks the cell adhesive alphaflem instructs the body to manufacture. We've manufactured enzymes to speed up the antibodies and transmission methods to target the brain. We've cured humankind. No more altereds." Before I could speak, he gestured for me to wait and continued, "And before you say it, bio-engineering departments are far greater than the rival electrical-engineering ones. Nano drone mastery won't prevent this cure, I assure you."

"So what next? Will you heal Autumn? What about the war?"

"You really are naïve, aren't you? I will have the neural net replaced, before the reckoning." He smirked.

"Reckoning?"

"All in good time, Mr Blue, all in good time." He waved a hand and turned. "I've had a few garments placed in the closet. I trust they will fit. An exodrone will be with you shortly. Listen and obey, and you'll have everything you could desire." He walked out the room repeating, "Everything you could desire." The doors slid back into place and locked shut; a thin red neon strip ran down the centre.

The closet had been stocked with Martian clothing. White tight-fitting robes and what's called a ruda, a fabric hood that when electrically charged would seal tight and provide a full face dust mask. Very expensive and highly sought after. I donned it all apart from the ruda, then sat and waited, staring out the window. I was Mappo's prisoner now.

My mind drifted to The Poet, the teachings he used to give me when I was younger. Stories of Master Koshi and Qen. The Poet would teach me how to meditate, correct my posture and instruct in what he called "the emptying phase". Distilling my thoughts to roots of feelings and then throwing those feelings out. Forgetting them and washing my mind clean with thoughtlessness.

But I was hindered. The Poet was the first altered Qen master. The first altered to reach satori and awaken views of earnest reality. He popularised the adoption of enhancements by publishing ten poems. Poems inspired by the Ox paintings from before the great African conflicts. Paintings thought to be lost. They were the articulation of what's called in Qen "chasing the self" and The Poet knew bringing anything Japanese to mainstream western media would catch plenty of attention. It was necessary, for a Qen master must "walk the path". And so he did.

The poems spread like wildfire. Rumour that evolved into myth spoke of people reading them and instantly reaching satori. There was a frenzy, The Poet instilled a scientific-moral thought system in what seemed like a day. Enhancements swept the lands, peace broke out amongst archaic rivals, world hunger vanished and happiness pervaded.

But some were left to creep behind. Inhibited by our genetics we crept, feeding from the tit of a higher post-humankind. And now Mappo was here to right the wrongs.

I took in a deep breath and exhaled sharply. My chest in motion from convex to concave, out then in, out then in. Ichi, ni, san, shi…

A vibration, shaken by a hand on my shoulder. My eyes opened, an exo. Trimmed with neon blue were plates of gold and black carbon steel. It had dark green lenses for eyes. It was what I would later find out to be a sentinel – a highly sophisticated drone. A seeker flew out from behind it and sprayed me with laser light. I winced.

"It's me. You don't have to confirm."

"This is not for that," the sentinel boomed. Waving the drone away, it continued, "Dr Nicholas Blue agreed to the terms set by Mr Elijah Mappo. We leaked memories from you and understand that Blue is working with the UANF. You are to be returned to Blue here and he will commence work on the SYX-Serum. At some point we suspect Blue will try to sabotage us by revealing locations of defence systems' control centres to UANF. Or by destroying the SYX-Serum growth tanks and deployment infrastructure. You must prevent that at all cost."

"What exactly are the terms he agreed to?" I said.

"Your life for his work."

"And what if I don't do as asked?"

"Creeps will forever answer to the altereds, Ms Autumn Flowers' neural net will be left to grow past the point of no return and a fierce battle will be fought on Phobos. You could end it before it started, save Flowers and rid the world of altereds."

Flowers, that was her last name, Flowers.

I ambled up to the window and rested my head once more. Staring out at the majestic giant I said, "I want a home, for me and for Autumn, a big one on the canals of Tharsis. And enough money for two lifetimes." I faced the sentinel. "Not creep lifetimes but altered lifetimes, 170 years' worth. Twice."

The sentinel's green lenses went dark. The soul had left the body. A moment later they beamed back to life. "Done. Now follow me, a buggy is waiting outside."

The doors split open and we marched down the hall. A gangway led down into a glass tunnel. I donned the ruda and stepped into the air chamber.

"Phobos has been leaking atmosphere," said the sentinel. "The ruda has been fitted with oxygen injectors. Breathe as normal but expect a little prick. I have no envy for you humans. Meat-sacks."

The ruda grew tight around me, jabbed at my neck on my right. A visor formed. Navigation and communication information scattered across my field of view. The air chamber sealed behind me and opened in front of me. I followed the sentinel out towards the buggy. Up high arching from the horizon I could see the faint outline of the mag-film as it flickered, like a twitching muscle fatigued and hungry for energy. It fought, desperate to contain as much atmosphere as possible. The Phobos gravel crunched under my feet, everything internal sounded louder or more focused. External sounds muffled and quieter, the sound of the buggy's engine spluttering to life.

Everything was so different to Earth.

Thirteen

The buggy rolled up to a vast crater rim. Phobos Prime's hangar, I never thought it could be this big. Peppered with tiny holes and small amounts of foliage, the rim had a circumference of what felt like miles. We stepped out and walked down a snake run towards the base of it. The climb up was quick. At the top an earthquake erupted, violent and sporadic. I stared into the sentinel's lenses, searching for some kind of humanity. Then the crater split, fractured right through the middle in a zigzag. The rumbling stopped. All the power now focused into moving these gigantic sides apart.

"What is this?" I screamed, dust and leaves flying everywhere.

"This is Payload. This is the new beginning," said the sentinel. A cranking, a methodical deep cranking followed by edges that appeared from the darkness of the crater. Purest white I'd ever seen. Curved edges appearing from the abyss. Two sides, as if you had taken two halves of a sphere and pushed them through each other.

The object started to bounce with light; it would glow then fade, glow then fade. Its essence almost divine, its size godly. It filled the crater and kept rising higher and higher.

"Blue is here," said the sentinel.

The Poet was here. From behind the object a small platform glided through the sky, suspended by wire and carried by larger seekers. As it came closer, I could see his wiry white hair flapping around. He was strapped tight to the platform, flat on his back. His hands and legs in restraints, a muzzle around his face.

"What's going on? Why is he restrained?"

Mappo's voice boomed out from the sentinel, "Ah, my dear Mr Blue, you honestly think I ever needed him?" The platform lowered by my feet. The Poet's face was torn and bloody. There was a large gouge in his thigh. "We've ripped the tracker out of him, taken the land-sats out from Phobos's orbit, no one can stop us. You, Mr Blue, are our saviour. Your genome was the last thing I needed. And now I will send Payload to Earth and cleanse it, rid it of the altereds. Yours is the Earth and everything that's in it, Mr Blue. One thing remains. Inject him with the SYX-Serum." The sentinel's wrist cocked and from it popped out a shooter. Its weight and size the same as my own. Cool metal. I wrapped my fist around the thing and with one last look at The Poet I fell to my knees and rammed the shooter into his chest.

Equals at last.

Fourteen

Forty-five years later I write this, alone, floating on the canals of Tharsis. Mappo gave me everything I asked for. But I'm still stuck at the crossroads. The Poet loved me; I never understood. Could never see past my bitterness. The Poet's work changed the world, but did he create that utopia? Mappo ripped it from him and now there's war and famine. We all started devolving the moment the altereds were wiped out.

    Whoever reads this: know that it was me. Zachary Elijah Blue, the man who brought the wrath of the ape down upon a world of humans. I will try to rebuild with worn out tools.

    Until sinew snaps.

Printed in Great Britain
by Amazon